Journey to Galumphagos

Seth Eisner

Illustrated by Ellen C. Maze

≈ *WindSide Alley Books* ≈

ISBN 9781491082324

Cover illustration by Ellen C. Maze – www.ellencmaze.com

Book design by Donnie Light – eBook76.com

Published by WindSide Alley Books, Tucson, AZ
windsidealleybooks@gmail.com

≈ *WindSide Alley Books* ≈

This book is dedicated to "Mom"

Many thanks to Barbara Croft – an accomplished fiction writer, scholar and teacher, and a better editor than I could have found for love or money; to Ruth Sterlin, a long-lost high school friend rediscovered just in time to help me with a bunch of solid suggestions; to Ellen Maze and Donnie Light, whose generosity exceeded the bounds of reason; and to my characters.

Part I. Journey to Galumphagos

Chapter 1. Leaving Home

Chloe Miller stood at her easel in the Rec Room. She drew yet another field of flowers. She was tired of drawing flowers, but adults liked them. They didn't seem to like much else she made. Yesterday, she wove a necklace from long pieces of dried grass.

"That looks scary, like a hangman's noose," her mother said. "Won't you draw me some pretty flowers?"

Jacob, Chloe's little brother, pranced around the easel practicing his Karate Katas for Kindergartners. Jacob practiced every day after school. His moves were getting so sure and swift that even the second and third graders didn't want to face him in a match.

But Jacob stumbled in the middle of a move and Chloe's blue crayon slipped across her drawing paper when their big sister Emily stormed into the Rec Room, threw her backpack in the corner, and hollered, "I've had it up to here!"

"Up to where?" said little brother Jacob.

"It's a figure of speech," said Chloe. "It means Emily's not happy."

"It means I'm angry!" said Emily.

"What about?" asked Jacob, but he already knew. Emily was the favorite target of a clique of popular kids at school.

"People," said Emily, "that's what! It's bad enough I have to eat lunch by myself every day. But today one of the cool girls 'stumbled' on my chair on purpose and spilled water all over my table. Then she ran off giggling, and all her friends giggled, too. I hate 'em, every one of 'em. People are a pain on the neck!"

"That's 'a pain *in* the neck,'" said Chloe.

"Oh yeah," said Emily. "I always get that one wrong. But that's beside the point. I've had it up to here with people, and I'm leaving. Forever!"

"Where will you go?" asked Jacob. "There are people everywhere."

"Oh, no, there aren't," said Emily. "Not on Galumphagos Island."

"Galumphagos Island is make-believe," said Jacob. "You can't really *go* there."

"Yes, you can," said Chloe, "but no one ever comes back."

"That's because they don't *want* to come back," said Emily, "because they like it better there. That's what all the travel brochures say." Emily waved a shiny travel brochure in front of Jacob. "Look. See? That's what it says right here."

"That's too much for Jacob to read," Chloe said.

That was true, but it wasn't too much for him to see. The pictures showed kids playing ball with galumphers on the beach, riding on the backs of Galumphagos Island tortoises, and swimming with Galumphagos Island turtles in the bay. Strange trees, beautiful flowers and colorful birds were in every picture. All the kids and animals were smiling and laughing. It looked wonderful.

"It says right here," Emily said, pointing to the brochure, "'Galumphagos Island sunfish jump right onto your plate where they clean and cook themselves for your culinary pleasure.'"

"What's 'culinary'?" Jacob asked.

"I don't know," said Emily. "Who cares? I'm going. Are you coming or are you not?"

Jacob stopped and thought. "I like people," he said.

"He likes everything," said Chloe.

"How about Norman and Oscar and Penelope?" asked Emily, but she already knew the answer.

Jacob didn't like any of those kids, especially Penelope. "Penelope's a pain on the neck," he said.

"Pain *in* the neck! Pain *in* the neck!" said Chloe.

"Oh yeah," said Jacob. "I always get that one wrong. What is a pain in the neck anyway?"

"It's a figure of speech," said Emily.

Something still bothered Jacob. "What about Mom and Dad?" he said.

Chloe shrugged at Emily and Emily shrugged back.

"Jacob," Chloe said, "I'm not sure we should tell you this. You're pretty little to know it already."

"But Mom and Dad are kinda useless," added Emily.

"Except for buying stuff."

"And we won't need to buy anything on Galumphagos Island."

Both sisters stared at Jacob. He hated it when they did that. He could never tell them "no" when they *both* stared at him at once.

Jacob stopped and thought. For every person he liked, he could think of one he didn't. For every nice thing a person had done, he could think of a nasty thing. As for Mom and Dad, well, Mom liked the girls better, and Dad's silly stories weren't funny anymore.

He looked at the travel brochures again. They were pretty. It must be nice to be on Galumphagos Island. Besides, Jacob couldn't imagine staying home if Emily and Chloe left. What would he do without them?

He decided to go.

They marched into the kitchen and announced to Mom and Dad, "We're going to Galumphagos Island."

"Oh no, you're not," said Dad. "Don't even think it."

"Now, dear," said Mom, "let's listen to what the children have to say. I'm sure they have their reasons for thinking they'd like to go."

"Yeah," said Emily. "Anywhere would be better than here. That's a good enough reason for me."

"It's boring here," said Chloe. "All anyone ever wants me to do is draw flowers."

"And what about you, young man?" Dad said to Jacob.

Jacob shrugged his shoulders. "Emily and Chloe are going," he said.

"But Mom and I aren't," Dad said. "What about us?"

Jacob shrugged his shoulders again and grabbed Emily's hand.

"The grass isn't always greener on the other side of the street," said Mom.

"What's that mean?" asked Jacob.

"It's a figure of speech," said Emily. "It means we might not like it any better there than we like it here."

"Well, like it or not, you're not going," said Dad, "and that's the final word!"

The kids knew it was useless to argue any more. So they went to bed, pretended they were asleep, and waited until it sounded like Mom and Dad were sleeping. They got up, emptied their piggy banks and packed their backpacks. Emily took some books, Chloe her crayons and some paper, and Jacob the football. They left their stuffed animals behind. The travel brochures said kids didn't need any stuffed animals on Galumphagos.

They tiptoed down the stairs and to the back door. Just in front of the door were three shopping bags. Each of their names was printed on one of the bags. A note was attached to Emily's. She opened it and read it to herself.

"What's it say?" asked Jacob.

Emily read it aloud but softly enough so she wouldn't wake Mom and Dad.

Dear Children,
I hope you won't go, but if you do, you will need some food. Here are some sandwiches. Your favorites – peanut butter on croissants. Be careful, children.
Love,

Mom

"There's more," Jacob said, looking over Emily's arm at the letter.

"I thought you couldn't read," said Emily.

"I can read 'Love' and 'Mom,'" he said, "and there's more writing underneath."

Chloe took the letter from Emily and read the rest of it. "Emily, I know this was your idea. You're in charge. Keep them safe!"

Chloe handed the letter back to Emily, who folded it neatly and put it into her backpack.

Then they left.

Chapter 2. Galumphagos Island

The only way to get to Galumphagos, or even to find it, is by paddleboat. No one knows why, but that's the way it is.

Emily, Chloe and Jacob bought a boat with their pooled savings and paddled their way across the 12 miles of Ocean between the Mainland and the Island. When they got there, they hid the paddleboat under some giant Galumphagos Island ferns.

Then they went looking for galumphers. Galumphers are everywhere on the Island, though they live nowhere else, and they are *huge*. The travel brochures said that the first galumphers had a brontosaurus for a dad and a teddy bear for a mom. They're big and clumsy and stupid, but they're also soft and furry and cuddly. That's why kids don't need stuffed animals when they go to the Island.

The brochures said no place is more fun than Galumphagos Island, and nothing is more fun than playing with galumphers. So that's exactly what the kids set out to do.

Jacob tried to play football with the galumphers.

"Hike the ball to me," he told a galumpher, "then run down the field. I'll throw a pass to you."

But when Jacob handed her the ball, she ran right over him and kept running.

"You're running the wrong way," Jacob yelled as loud as he could. But none of the galumphers paid any attention at all. They all chased the galumpher with the ball and shouted, all together, "Knock'EmDown-Knock'Em Down-Knock'Em Down." They smashed into each other and sometimes into Jacob, who always got knocked flying. Most of the time, Jacob had no idea where the ball was, and it didn't seem to matter anyway. The game was more like a big wrestling match than football.

"That's not football!" Jacob said.

"Of course not," said a galumpher. "It's Galumphutball." Then he ran right over Jacob, too.

In not very long at all, a wrestling galumpher fell on the ball and squashed it flat.

"Uh-oh," said the galumpher.

"Penelope," another galumpher yelled at her, "you always squash the ball!"

"Game over," said a third.

They really are big, thought Jacob, looking sadly at what used to be his football and at the bruises on his arms and legs.

Chloe tried to show the galumphers how to draw. She handed out crayons and paper, then sat down to start drawing herself.

"What should we draw?" she asked, but none of the galumphers answered. "There are strange and beautiful plants here. Let's draw them."

But the galumphers drew pictures of nothing. Their drawings were just bunches of scribbles and squiggles. Even the grown-up galumphers drew like two year-old children.

Then they all started screaming, over and over again, "PressVeryHard-PressVeryHard-PressVeryHard." Her crayons broke in half, then broke in half again.

"Stop," Chloe yelled as loud as she could, "that's not drawing. And you're wrecking all my crayons." But none of the galumphers paid any attention. In not very long at all, they broke every crayon into pieces so small that Chloe couldn't even hold them in her fingers.

They really are clumsy, thought Chloe, looking sadly at the pile of rubbish that used to be her crayons.

Emily sat down to read. "Shall we have some stories?" she asked some little galumphers.

"Oh yes," said the galumphers. "Do you want to tell your stories or should we tell ours?"

Emily, who loved to read and was already missing her books, said "I'll tell you a story," and opened the book in her lap.

The little galumphers covered their ears and hollered "NoReading-NoReading-NoReading."

"Why not?" asked Emily.

"It's not allowed," said one little galumpher.

"Then what do you do for stories?" asked Emily.

"We tell them," said a galumpher. "Like this. There was a galumpher and she burped."

All the galumphers laughed and laughed. One said "I liked that one," and another said "That was really good."

"Two galumphers," said another, "bumped into each other and fell down." The galumphers loved that story, too.

"Those aren't stories," said Emily. But none of the galumphers paid any attention at all, and soon one of the little galumphers grabbed Emily's book and ate it.

They really are stupid, thought Emily, looking on sadly as her book turned into lunch.

When the kids were back together that night, Emily said, "Aren't we having fun!"

Jacob stopped and thought, but he didn't say anything.

Chloe said, "Let's hit the sack."

"What sack?" asked Jacob.

"Oh!" said Emily, "It's just a figure…"

Before Emily could finish her sentence, two galumphers flashed into view. One wore boxing gloves. The other tucked its arms and legs into itself so it looked like a big furry sack with a head. The first started punching the second. With every punch, the first said, "Hit" and the second said "the sack."

"Hit…" – punch…

"… the sack."

"Hit…" – punch…

"… the sack."

"Hit…" – punch…

"… the sack."

Then the sack-galumpher stood right in front of Jacob, ready to be hit some more.

Emily took her little brother by the hand and walked him away. "No thanks, Mr. Galumpher," she said. "We're tired."

Chapter 3. The Grass Isn't Greener

The next morning, the kids found a GalumphaBird. Emily looked it up in the brochure. "GalumphaBirds are the funniest things on earth," it said. "They'll leave you in stitches!"

"What's 'leave you in stitches' mean?" Jacob asked.

"It's a figure of speech," said Chloe. "It means they're so funny that your side will hurt from laughing so hard."

The GalumphaBird's wings were so short that it could hardly fly, but it flapped them very fast so that it could jump and stay up in the air for just a little while. It was a pretty combination of green and blue. Chloe thought it would be fun to draw a picture of it if her crayons hadn't been wrecked.

"Hello, GalumphaBird," said Jacob. "Do something funny."

Chloe held her finger out so the bird could land on it. The GalumphaBird jumped toward Chloe's hand but, instead of landing on it, bit her finger and wouldn't let go.

"Ow, ow, ow!" said Chloe. "Help me, help me!"

A dozen galumphers flashed into view. They pointed at Chloe, laughed aloud and said, over and over again, "Isn'tThatFunny-Isn'tThatFunny-Isn'tThatFunny."

Two of them, both dressed in white jackets like doctors, pulled the GalumphaBird's tail feathers until it let go of Chloe's hand. Then they took needles and thread out of their jacket pockets and said, "LeaveInStitches-LeaveInStitches-LeaveInStitches."

Emily pulled Chloe away. "I'll bandage it," she said. "I brought some stuff from home." Emily cleaned the cut, put some ointment on it, and covered it with a Band-Aid.

"Does it feel better?" Emily asked.

"It hurts!" Chloe shouted. She glared at the galumphers, but that just seemed to make them laugh even louder.

Then the kids found a Galumphagos Island Tortoise. *What harm could a tortoise do*? they thought. Jacob climbed on its back to go for a ride. It seemed nice at first, but soon the Tortoise started bucking like a rodeo bronco. Then it stood on one of its hind legs and spun around like a figure skater. Jacob went flying off and crashed into a tree.

"Ouch," he said. "Why'd you do that, you stupid tortoise?"

Again, galumphers flashed into view from somewhere or other, laughing and pointing their fingers as they all shouted "BigBadBruise-BigBadBruise-BigBadBruise."

Emily didn't think that their laughter looked or sounded happy. It looked like a smirk and sounded like a snicker.

* * *

The next day, the kids found the same Galumphagos Island Tortoise. "Can I have another ride, Mr. Tortoise?" Jacob asked.

"Jacob," Emily said, "what are you doing? You'll get hurt again."

He winked at her, got on the tortoise and took another ride. The result was the same. Jacob got thrown into a tree. Again, galumphers flashed up from nowhere, laughing.

Jacob walked toward the tortoise, a smile on his face, and took a deep karate bow. The tortoise got up on its hind legs and began to imitate him, but before it got half way into its bow, Jacob gave it his very best kick, right in the belly.

The tortoise groaned, fell down, and pulled its head, legs and tail inside its shell. Jacob backed up, took a running start, leaped and landed so hard on the tortoise's back that its head, feet and tail popped back out of its shell. "Ugh!" said the tortoise.

Jacob and Chloe pointed at the tortoise and laughed. "Isn'tThatFunny-Isn'tThatFunny-Isn'tThatFunny," they said to each other again and again. Galumphers flashed into view saying exactly the same thing.

Then Chloe waved to the GalumphaBird and said, "Oh, pretty bird, won't you visit me again?"

"Chloe," Emily said, "do you want to be left in stitches again?"

Chloe winked. The bird jumped right toward her nose, but Chloe was ready this time. She had woven a noose from shreds of tree bark and was holding it behind her back. Just before the GalumphaBird was about to land on her nose, she lassoed the bird, pulled the noose tight, and swung the bird around and around and around over her head.

"Isn'tThatFunny-Isn'tThatFunny-Isn'tThatFunny," Chloe and Jacob screamed. Chloe kept swinging the bird around.

Emily looked at the nearby galumphers. She expected them to be angry, but instead they were laughing just as they had yesterday, with that nasty, smirky kind of laugh. It reminded her of the girls at school.

"Stop!" Emily screamed. "Chloe, let that bird go!"

"Why?" Chloe screamed back as she kept swinging the GalumphaBird. "If it bit you the way it bit me, you'd do the same thing."

"I wouldn't kill it," Emily said.

Chloe stopped to take a look. Emily was right. The bird would die if Chloe kept swinging it. She loosened the noose and let the bird go, but she was still angry.

"What are you two doing?" Emily said.

"We're just defending ourselves," said Chloe.

"Getting even," said Jacob, with a smirk on his face.

"Do you want to wind up being like them?" Emily said.

"Who are you to talk?" said Chloe. "You're the one who dragged us here."

"And we're the ones getting hurt," said Jacob.

"Maybe people aren't so great," said Chloe.

"But galumphers are worse!" said Jacob.

They stood without even looking at each other. They were all angry, but they weren't sure whom they were angry at.

"I guess the grass *isn't* greener on the other side of the street," Emily finally said.

"Or the other side of the Ocean," said Chloe.

Emily nodded. "Okay," she said, "let's call it a day."

Two galumphers flashed into view. One pointed at a rock and said "It," and the other said "a day." Saying something once was never enough for the galumphers, so they kept saying it again and again and again.

Emily finally got angry and said, "Zip your stupid lips!"

Suddenly, zippers appeared on the galumphers' mouths and each zipped up the other's lips.

The three kids gave each other the "shush" sign – an index finger across the lips. If they said anything at all, it seemed, they might use a figure of speech, and that would give the galumphers an excuse to flash into view and do something crazy.

Chapter 4. Eating Mush

From that time on, galumphers were nearby almost all the time. The kids hardly had a waking moment to themselves. When they thought they were alone, a galumpher would appear as if it had just popped out of the ground. Galumphers had an odd way of showing up.

"Let's play and cuddle!" they'd say. But "cuddling" from a galumpher felt more like wrestling. When galumphers played, they ran around in circles and zigzags and figure eights, hollering "WannaPlay-WannaPlay-WannaPlay," like it was all one word. They bumped into the children again and again and knocked them down like they were bowling pins.

"You Miller kids fall down too much. You need to get big and strong like us," the galumphers told them. "You should eat mush, just like we do."

Galumphagos Island mush was the only food the galumphers ate. It looked awful and smelled worse. The kids did not want to eat it, but the galumphers kept telling them that they should.

"Does it taste like broccoli?" asked Jacob.

"Oh no!" said the galumphers, "You don't have to worry about that!"

"He likes broccoli," said Chloe.

"Does it taste like peas?" asked Emily.

The galumphers were smarter this time. "Oh yes," they said.

"She hates peas," said Chloe.

Finally, Chloe — who will taste almost anything and likes more than she doesn't — said, "How bad can it be? Give me a taste, please."

It was awful. Chloe spit it out all over the place.

The galumphers looked like their feelings were hurt. They tried to make the kids feel guilty for not eating mush.

No matter what the galumphers said, though, none of the children would eat mush. They kept eating peanut butter sandwiches until they ran out. After that, they ate fish when they could catch them. When they couldn't, they ate fruits and nuts and berries, until Jacob got a loose caboose.

But none of the kids said that figure of speech out loud. Who knew what a galumpher might do if someone said "loose caboose"?

Chapter 5. Special Delivery

The next evening, a Great Galumphagos Island Turtle waddled onto the beach, stood on its hind legs and waved to the children. The children didn't know if the sea turtle would be any nicer than the tortoise, but they took a chance and walked up to it.

The turtle held something in its front foot. "Special Delivery," it said, dropped something on the sand, and waddled back into the Ocean.

The kids ran to see what the turtle had dropped. It was a letter. They tore the envelope open. Emily read the letter aloud when they had a few minutes alone, with no galumphers looking or listening.

Dear Children,

How are you? We hope the galumphers are treating you well. Don't forget to brush your teeth and to wear your boots when it rains.

We are very lonely. We hope you'll change your minds and come home. Your beds are made, and there's still peanut butter in the jar. We froze the croissants. Write us if you decide to come home, and we'll defrost them.

Things aren't the same here without you. When you were here, we always had too much to do and too little time. Now there's too much time, and we don't know what to do with it.

We liked it better the other way.

Love,

Mom and Dad

Jacob stopped and thought about Mom and Dad, but he refused to let himself cry.

Chloe wondered whether you *could* go home from Galumphagos Island.

And Emily had to admit that the journey to Galumphagos was not what she had hoped it would be. She didn't like galumphers any better than she liked people.

In fact, she missed people, even though many had been unkind to her. She missed Mom and Dad and her teachers and even a few of the kids at school. They weren't all mean. Maybe she'd ask some of them to eat lunch with her when she got back.

If she got back.

"Well, I think our toothbrushes are lost, but I guess it's time to go to sleep," Emily said. "I'll tuck you both in."

And she did. Chloe, who thought she was too big to be tucked in, didn't even try to stop her.

Chapter 6. Escape

The galumphers started staying with them even when they slept. "Since you didn't bring any stuffed animals," the galumphers would say, "don't you want to cuddle with us?" Even if the children said *no*, a galumpher would sleep nearby.

Emily awoke one morning when it was just beginning to turn light. She had an itch on her right arm. She scratched it. The spot that itched was soft and furry. She stared at it. It was the same golden color and about the same length as galumpher hair.

She checked out Chloe and Jacob, who were still asleep. Chloe had a furry spot on her leg and Jacob had one on his neck, all the same color and about the length of a bear's hair.

"Chloe," she whispered, after making sure the nearby galumpher was still asleep. "Wake up. Jacob, get up." She gave each of them the "shush" sign.

"Feel your left leg, Chloe," whispered Emily, "below your knee. Jacob, feel the back of your neck."

"What is it?" Jacob asked.

"It's fur," Chloe whispered. "We're growing fur."

"Golden fur, like the galumphers. We're becoming stupid, too," said Emily. "I can't remember the last time I read a book or even wanted to."

"Did I do karate practice?" asked Jacob.

"I lost my crayons," said Chloe. "And I feel like I want to be mean all the time."

"And pretty soon we'll have to eat mush," said Emily. "We won't have anything else."

Emily went to the pile of things she had brought with her from the Mainland. She pulled out a travel brochure and held it up. The brochure said galumphers were so much fun that kids never wanted to leave, and that was why none ever came back from the Island.

But they all knew better now. The real reason kids didn't come back was because they weren't kids any more. They turned into galumphers – big, clumsy, stupid and mean.

The children looked at each other. All at once, they whispered, "We're turning into galumphers!"

They knew the truth now, but was it too late? They had to escape from Galumphagos, but how? With the galumphers watching them all the time, they hardly had a chance even to make an escape plan.

They watched carefully for a few moments when they could speak to each other in secret. When they finally got their chance, they made their plan.

"I'll..." said Emily, and she silently pretended she was singing a song.

"And I'll…" said Chloe, wiggling her fingers.

"And I'll…" said Jacob, rubbing his right fist into the palm of his left hand.

A galumpher was with them that night at bedtime.

"We haven't had a bedtime story since we've been here," said Emily. "Chloe and Jacob, would you like a story?"

"You're not going to *read* a story," said the galumpher, "are you?"

"Read!!!" said Emily. "Yuck! Of course not. I'll *tell* a story."

"Phew!" said the galumpher. "That's better."

"Let's all cuddle up here," said Emily. "First I'll sing a lullaby."

Emily sang softly and slowly, and Chloe gently rubbed the galumpher's back. The galumpher let his head droop, said "Ahhhh," and closed his eyes.

While Emily continued to croon and Chloe continued to massage, Jacob snuck up behind the galumpher and leapt high. As he came down, Jacob karate chopped the galumpher right on the top of the head and knocked her out cold.

The children ran like mad for the shore. But when they got there, their paddleboat was missing.

"It's a good thing we're all such good swimmers," Chloe said. "Twelve miles — that's nothing."

They ran into the Ocean and swam. And swam. And swam. Twelve miles was a lot more Ocean than they thought it would be. They still had a long, long way to go when Jacob couldn't swim any further. He started to tread water.

Emily swam close by to help him stay up.

Chloe, the strongest swimmer, was in the lead. She turned around and came back. They held hands together and kicked underwater to stay afloat.

"What do we do now?" Jacob asked.

No one had an answer. They just held onto each other and kept bobbing in the water.

"I'm sorry," Emily said. "This is all my fault. I don't think we're going to get back to...." Before she could finish the sentence, three great mounds rose from the sea, one under each of them.

"Hold onto our backs, children," said the largest mound of the three, which carried Emily.

The children were exhausted. They huffed and puffed for a long time while their mounds swam silently along in the direction of the Mainland.

"May I ask," Emily finally said, "on whose back I have the privilege of riding?"

"Nicely phrased, my dear," said Emily's mound. "You are a passenger on The Great Galumphagos Island Turtle. That is I. Chloe rides aback my daughter, The Not-Yet-Great Galumphagos Island Turtle, and Jacob upon my husband, The Not-So-Great Galumphagos Island Turtle. Since Galumphagos Island Turtle is such a lot to say, we usually call ourselves GITs. I hope you won't mind."

"We don't mind at all," Emily said, "but how do you know our names?"

"Oh, we GITs live a very long time, and we've been watching the Island nearly all our lives, hoping for our chance to help. We have watched you ever since you arrived, and here you are. You are very brave, my dears. You are the first ever to try to escape. And you shall succeed – we GITs shall see to that."

"Did you bring us Mommy's and Daddy's letter?" Jacob asked.

"*I* did," said the Not-Yet-Great GIT.

"Thank you," said Chloe. "It must have been hard for you to come all that way up the beach."

"Not nearly as hard as it is for you to swim across the Ocean," said the Great GIT. "But enough talking. You children must be very tired. Please rest and enjoy the ride."

Chapter 7. Home Again

When they reached the Mainland, the children asked the GITs to come to their home for dinner.

"Most kind of you," said The Great GIT, "but we don't eat peanut butter. Besides, we have another letter to deliver."

They thanked the GITs again and again. "I guess there's good and bad wherever you go, Ms. Great GIT," Emily said. "If we hadn't met the three of you, I would have thought Galumphagos Island was *all* bad."

At long last, the children arrived at the door of their house. Mom and Dad sat at the kitchen table, eating dinner. They weren't really eating. They just sat there, slumping and looking very sad.

"I wish the kids would come home," said Mom. "I love them so."

"I really miss them," said Dad. "This is worse than when Emily went away to overnight camp."

Then Mom started to cry, and the kids just couldn't stand it anymore. They burst into the room, all screaming at the same time, "Mom, Dad, we're home."

Everyone hugged and kissed and laughed and cried, all at the same time.

Then they did it all over again.

Finally, it was quiet for a moment. They all smiled at each other without saying a word until Dad asked, "How'd you like the galumphers?"

"They're a pain on the neck," Jacob said.

"Pain *in* the neck," said Emily and Chloe together, "pain *in* the neck."

Part II. Revenge of the Galumphers

Chapter 8. Invasion

Emily sat alone in the Rec Room watching the 5 P.M. news.

"A fleet of paddleboats is approaching the Mainland," TV newsman Eddie Exposure reported. "The Coast Guard checked out the boats! Reports are Top Secret, but here at Channel Umpteen News – News on the Spot that Hits the

Spot – we think that the paddleboats may carry an army of galumphers. Let's go to our reporter on the spot, Delia DeFogger."

The newscast shifted to the shore of the Mainland.

"We can see the paddleboats for sure," said Delia DeFogger. "Thousands of them are coming our way fast, but it's hard to see what's in them. Every once in a while, we'll catch a glimpse of two creatures that look like galumphers. They're side-by-side in a boat, pedaling like mad with grimaces on their faces. Then, in a flash, they disappear. Pop, we see them, pop, we don't, like flashbulbs going off in the dark. The boats keep moving toward us, but we're not sure who's pedaling them."

The camera moved back to the newsroom and Eddie Exposure.

"Meanwhile, on the beaches of the Mainland," Eddie said, "children are gathering to welcome the galumphers as if Santa himself was coming to town. As everyone knows, galumphers are soft, furry, cuddly and lovable, and more fun to play with than action figures. The kids just can't wait!"

The camera shifted again. The TV now showed thousands of kids and parents on the beach holding hand-made signs that said, "We love galumphers" and "Bring 'em on." People jostled each other to get in front of the camera. "I WannaplayWannaplayWannaplay," said one fat five-year old who was eating a triple-scoop ice cream cone.

"So that's the story," Eddie concluded. "Stay with us for non-stop coverage of this exciting event! We're waiting for galumphers, and we're gonna have fun!"

"Shows how much *they* know," Emily said just as Chloe, Jacob and Mom entered the room and joined her in front of the TV.

"What's going on?" asked Mom.

"Just watch," said Emily.

Police guards lined the shore as the fleet of paddleboats pounded through the surf and approached the Mainland. The Mayor stood on the shore next to Delia DeFogger.

"So, Mayor," asked Delia, "what gives with all the fuzz here?"

The Mayor looked confused. "I think you must be mistaken, Delia," he said. "Galumphers are furry, not fuzzy."

"Sorry, Boss Man," said Delia, "I was using a figure of speech I guess you're not familiar with. Let me rephrase my question. Why are all the police here?"

"Well, Delia," the Mayor said, "we all know the galumphers are soft and furry and cuddly, and we sure want the kids to have a great time. But with all these children here, and all the galumphers coming – at least we think they're galumphers, and we think they're coming – we just want to make sure that everyone's safe." The Mayor beamed a fatherly smile at the TV cameras.

Within moments, line after line of paddleboats crashed onto the shore and jerked to stops.

"Here they are," exclaimed Delia in a booming voice, "and we're gonna have barrels of fun."

Then the broadcast stopped, as if the power had been knocked out. Mom, Emily, Chloe and Jacob saw a fuzzy pattern and heard a buzz on the TV. When the sound and picture came back, a minute later, the Mayor was still standing in front of the camera.

"Oddest thing I've ever seen," the Mayor said to Delia DeFogger. "The landing craft hit the beach, and then we heard feet pounding on the sand. Well, I don't know if they were feet or paws or hooves or whatever, but they sure pounded. It sounded like an earthquake, and felt like one, too, but you couldn't see a thing. Well, hardly a thing. Every once in a while one or two would flash into view, and then just as fast they'd disappear.

"Then we saw thousands of furry barrels rolling up the beach as fast as cars. They shouted 'barrels of fun, barrels of fun' over and over again. They banged into the kids and knocked them around like bowling pins. There were as many parents on the beach as kids, but the barrels hardly hit a single adult. Just the kids. We got kids banged up and crying all over the beach.

"Then it was all over. The landing craft are still there, but the invaders — galumphers or whatever they were — are nowhere to be seen."

"Invaders, Mayor?" Delia asked. "Landing craft? Those are paddleboats, aren't they? The kind that kids like to paddle, and they probably had soft, cuddly galumphers in them – right?"

"That may be so, Delia," said the Mayor. "But make no mistake about it. This was an attack on the Mainland! There were thousands of them storming and stomping and rolling up the beach. Then they were gone. We don't know where. We don't know what their target is. But we're telling all Mainlanders to be careful. It could be dangerous out there."

"Of course, Mayor," said Delia, smirking just like a galumpher. "Everyone knows how dangerous galumphers are! Why, they're even more dangerous than teddy bears."

Back in the Rec Room, Chloe said, "Shows how much *she* knows!"

Chapter 9. Target

Dad came into the Rec Room. "This is unusual," he said. "All four of you in front of the TV together. What's up?"

"Haven't you heard?" said Mom. "We're being invaded!"

"Invaded? Where? How? Who?"

"No one knows," said Mom. "They're kind of invisible." Then she explained about the fleets of paddleboats and the kids on the beach and the Mayor.

Emily, Chloe and Jacob said in unison, "It's the galumphers."

"How can you be so sure?" asked Dad.

The kids stared at Dad.

"Oh," he said. "Right. You'd know."

"I don't know what they're doing here," said Emily. "Has it ever happened before?"

Mom and Dad said no. As far as they knew, the galumphers had never come to the Mainland.

"Well, I've had enough of them!" said Chloe. "Whatever they're doing here, they're not going to do it with me."

"But what if they're coming for *us*?" asked Jacob with a frightened look on his face.

Emily's eyes widened, and her mouth opened to make an *O*. "They could be," she said.

"We escaped," said Chloe. "That's never happened before. No one ever came back from the Island before."

"Then they came over from the Island to the Mainland," said Mom. "That's never happened before either."

"They're angry," said Emily. "They wanted us to be just like them. We didn't want to and got away. They might want to capture us and take us back to the Island."

They all sat back down in front of the TV.

"It's been hard for the police to spot them," said Delia DeFogger. "We can only see them once in a while. They're invisible most of the time. But the Police have been doing their best to keep track of the sightings when the galumphers do flash into view.

"They've given all that information to the Mainland's greatest mathematician, Professor Epperson Chuckles of Mainland Tech University. Professor Chuckles will try to figure out where the galumphers are heading. We're here with the Professor in his classroom."

Professor Chuckles stood in front of a huge chalkboard with numbers and drawings all over it. It looked like a maze, or maybe just a mess.

"It's perfectly clear," said Professor Chuckles. "The galumphers' movements seem random, but I, Professor Epperson Chuckles, the Mainland's and perhaps even the world's greatest mathematician, figured out that the galumphers are heading to this spot, right here." The Professor pointed to a spot in the middle of the maze of scrawls on the chalkboard.

"Let me see, Professor Epperson Chuckles, Maestro of Mathematics," said Delia DeFogger. "That's a dot in the middle of a mess of scribbles. Is that correct?"

"In fact, Ms. DeFogger, as you would see if you knew your math, that is 220 WindSide Lane in Mainland Village."

The Miller family had a name for 220 WindSide Lane. They called it "home."

Chapter 10. Capture

As the minutes ticked away, it became clear that Professor Chuckles was right. The galumphers were moving closer and closer to the Miller's family home. Then the galumphers were at their home. They bumped into each other and banged into the doors and windows. When they flashed into view, they looked furious.

"We have to capture one," said Chloe.

"To interrogate," said Jacob, proud of himself for using such a big word.

"And to make it tell us what they're doing here, and what their plan is," added Emily.

"But even if we could capture one," said Mom, "how would we make it tell us their plan?"

Jacob swiftly moved into a karate Kama. "We'll beat it out of 'im," he said.

"Don't you even think it," said Mom, "not in our home!"

Jacob dropped his fighting stance.

"We'll find a way," said Emily.

"But how can we catch just one," asked Dad, "without having hundreds run into the house and tear everything up?"

"We need a diversion," said Chloe.

"Yes... we... do," said Emily. Both sisters stared at Jacob.

"Oh no!" said Jacob. "They're both staring at *me* again!"

"But the galumphers are after *us*," said Emily, "not Mom and Dad. So *we* have to be the diversion."

"And you're the one they'll want most, Jacob," said Chloe.

"Why?" he demanded. "You and Emily escaped, too."

"But you conked 'er a good one, Jacob," said Emily.

Jacob slumped. There was no way around it. There never was when Emily and Chloe *agreed* on something, which fortunately didn't happen too often. "Okayyyyyy," he said, "what's the plan?"

"You'll stand in front of the sliding glass doors at the back of the house," said Emily.

"Emily and I will stand on the sides and open the drapes so the galumphers will see you," said Chloe.

"Then you'll taunt them," said Emily. "You'll be like Earthworm in *James and the Giant Peach*. You'll tempt the galumphers into our web."

"They'll get really wild and crazy," said Chloe. "Then Emily and I will pull the drapes shut for a few seconds."

"Then we'll do it all over again."

"But how will we capture a galumpher that way?" asked Dad.

"We won't," said Chloe.

"That's just the diversion," said Emily. "After we do that a few times, almost all the galumphers will be in the back yard trying to get at Jacob. We'll know for sure because they'll be clumped together so closely that we'll see bunches of them."

"But a few slower ones will still be near the front door," said Chloe.

"Mom and Dad," said Jacob, who knew by now what was coming next. "You should sit down to hear the rest of this."

Mom and Dad sat down. They looked very confused.

"After we give you the signal that almost all of them are in the back yard," Chloe said…

"Dad, you'll have to open the front door but just about half way," said Emily.

"Then, Mom, as soon as you know that one's inside," said Chloe, "you have to put your shoulder to the door, slam it shut as hard as you can, and lock it."

"But they're invisible," said Mom. "How will I know when one is inside?"

"You'll know," said Jacob.

Emily put her hand on Dad's arm. "Dad," she said, "you might want to put your bicycle helmet on."

"And put a few pillows on the floor near the door," said Chloe.

"Wait a minute," said Jacob. He ran upstairs then came back in a flash, wearing his Karate Gi and carrying some pillows. "Ready?" he asked as he threw the pillows on the floor near the front door.

"Ready," said Emily and Chloe together, and the three of them leapt into a flying, three-way high-five.

Mom and Dad looked on, mouths gaping. "What happened to our innocent little children?" asked Mom.

"They went to Galumphagos Island," said Dad.

"And," said Jacob,

"Came," said Chloe,

"Back!" concluded Emily.

A round of "awrights," "Oh yeahs" and "cools" echoed through the house, followed by another flying triple high-five.

"*Stations!*" ordered Emily. The kids ran to the back of the house by the sliding glass door. Mom and Dad took their positions by the front door. Dad was wearing his bicycle helmet.

Emily and Chloe slowly opened the drapes. Jacob stood in front of the glass doors. He bowed slowly, and then started doing karate kicks and punches. The galumphers started heading to the door. There were so many of them that they were flashing into and out of view every second.

"Now!" said Emily, and she and Chloe quickly pulled the drapes closed.

"Let's do it again," said Jacob.

They opened the drapes again. Now there were even more galumphers. Jacob pointed at them and laughed out loud. He acted like he was laughing so hard that he had to double over. "I'm in stitches," he said as loud as he could.

The galumphers got madder and madder. Some got so angry they forgot there was a glass door between them and their target. They ran into the door and knocked themselves senseless.

Emily and Chloe closed the drapes fast again.

"One more time," said Chloe.

"Mom and Dad," said Emily, "this should do it. Be ready."

"When we say *GO*," said Jacob...

"...you *GO!*" finished Chloe.

When Emily and Chloe opened the drapes this time, Jacob started blowing kisses at the galumphers. There were piles of knocked-out galumphers by the door. They looked like a big pile of fur.

"GO!" yelled the kids, and Emily and Chloe closed the drapes again.

Dad opened the door and was knocked flying. Mom slammed the door shut and locked it.

"It knocked me for a loop!" said Dad.

"LoopLoopLoopLoop" screamed the galumpher again and again. Everyone could see it all the time since it came into the house. They watched as it spun in loops like a figure skater, crashing into everyone and everything.

"Oh dear," said Mom, "another lamp! Oh no, not grandmother's crystal vase." Then Mom herself got knocked for a loop, but she didn't say a word about it.

Before long, the house looked like a tornado had come through it. Just about anything that could be broken was. The sound of the galumpher's heavy clomps echoed through the house.

"We forgot to tell you," said Emily. "No figures of speech!"

"Galumphers make them real," said Jacob.

"Say it plain," said Chloe.

"I don't know if I can," said Dad, who was just getting up from the floor and heading to his favorite chair.

"Just do your best, Dad," Jacob said. "That's all we can ask."

Chapter 11. Peanut Butter

Dad grunted "ooooomfff" as the galumpher finally grew tired of running around and jumped onto his lap.

"WannaEatMushWannaEatMushWannaEatMush!" the galumpher hollered.

"We don't have any," gasped Dad, trying to catch his breath.

"GottaGoGottaGoGottaGo!" the galumpher screamed.

"I'm afraid you can't," said Dad. He hung on tight, but the galumpher struggled to get free.

Jacob, still wearing his Karate Gi, stood in front of the galumpher. He struck a fighting stance.

"You've heard the story of how we escaped?" said Emily. The little galumpher stopped squirming and nodded.

"Then stay put," said Jacob. He remained in his stance.

"What else would you like to eat, little galumpher?" Mom said in her sweetest voice.

"You wouldn't call it little if it had jumped in your lap," said Dad,

Mom gave him a sharp look.

"Mush," the galumpher said. "WannaEat Mush."

"We don't have mush," Mom said, "but we do have peanut butter sandwiches."

"It's not allowed," the galumpher said.

"Says who?" demanded Dad.

"Everybody!" said the galumpher.

"Well, I'm somebody," Dad argued back, "and I don't say."

"Me neither!" added Jacob.

Mom shushed them both. Mom always said you get more from kids with sugar than with scolding, and this galumpher seemed like a kid.

"You're right, little galumpher," Mom said sweetly. "That's the rule on the Island, and you're a good galumpher to follow the rule. But we have different rules here."

"That's right," said Emily, trying to sound just like Mom. "Here on the Mainland, the Moms and Dads make the rules."

"And we say it's just fine to eat peanut butter sandwiches," said Mom.

The galumpher looked up at Dad, as if he had the last word on anything. *Shows how much it knows*, thought Dad, but he said, "That's right. It's good to eat peanut butter sandwiches here."

So the galumpher said yes. Mom rushed into the kitchen to make a peanut butter sandwich on a croissant.

The little galumpher took the first bite of the sandwich, said "Oooh, that's so yummy," swayed back and forth, and began to cry for joy. But it didn't cry tears and didn't cry just from its eyes. It cried fur. It cried fur from all over itself, all of its fur, piles of it on Dad and on the chair and on the floor.

As the fur fell, its front paws turned into hands, its back paws into feet, and the galumpher into a little girl, about six years old from the look of her.

Everyone in the family stared at the little girl, then stared at each other, then – all at the same time – shouted "*Stations!*" and went running.

Mom and Emily ran into the kitchen and started making peanut butter sandwiches as fast as they could.

Chloe, the fastest runner, ran to get a big tray and sped back into the kitchen. She waited for Mom and Emily to load sandwiches onto the tray.

Jacob, the best thrower, ran upstairs. "I'll throw the sandwiches out the back window," he yelled.

Dad ran to the phone and dialed the police. "Police?" he said. "This is Sam Miller at 220 WindSide Lane."

"Here's one," said Mom, and she put a sandwich on Chloe's tray.

"What do you mean spell my name? This is 220 WindSide Lane, where all the galumphers are."

"Here's another," said Emily.

Chloe took off to give the sandwiches to Jacob.

"Will you stop asking stupid questions? We have the solution to the invasion!"

"Mush!" Jacob screamed out the open window. "Here's mush!" He threw the sandwiches to the galumphers.

Chloe ran back into the kitchen. "Do you have any more ready?"

"Let's make one-sided sandwiches," said Emily. "That'll be faster, and our supplies will last longer." She handed Chloe three one-sided sandwiches while Mom handed her two two-sided sandwiches.

"Put the Chief on the phone right now!" Dad demanded in his most impressive voice.

Chloe ran back upstairs with the five new sandwiches.

"It's working," said Jacob.

Chloe ran back to the kitchen and relayed Jacob's message.

"How about the one-sided sandwiches?" asked Mom. "Do they work, too?"

"I'll ask Jacob as soon as I'm back upstairs."

"Chief, send the helicopters to drop thousands of peanut butter sandwiches at 220 WindSide Lane, ASAP!"

"On croissants," said Mom.

"On croissants," Dad repeated into the phone.

The little galumpher who was now a little girl wandered into the kitchen. "Where are my mommy and daddy?" she asked.

"One-sided works, too," said Jacob when Chloe arrived with next load of sandwiches. Chloe again relayed the message into the noisy, frenzied kitchen.

"One-sided will do, Chief."

"We'll find them for you in a little while, honey, okay?" said Mom.

The little girl nodded. Dad picked her up and sat her down on the counter where Mom and Emily were making sandwiches.

"The Chief wants to know if it has to be croissants."

"We're not sure," said Emily, "but we know it works that way."

"If it ain't broke," said Mom, "don't fix it."

"Croissants if you got 'em, Chief!"

Dad hung up the phone and joined in the sandwich making. "We're out of croissants," he said.

"Try bread," Mom said.

"And cut them in half," said Emily. "Maybe all they need is a bite of peanut butter."

They went through three jumbo-sized jars of peanut butter and all the croissants, bread and rolls they had in the house. Then they started using crackers.

Emily was right. It didn't matter what they put the peanut butter on. Galumphers turned into children as soon as they took a bite.

By the time they ran out, Mom, Dad and Emily couldn't have lifted their arms to scrape any more peanut butter out of the jar, Chloe couldn't have run up and down the stairs one more time, and Jacob couldn't have made one more throw.

"The 'copters are coming!" yelled Jacob as he ran downstairs to join the rest of the family.

Parachutists jumped from the helicopters, each carrying a large box of sandwiches. They started to toss sandwiches to the galumphers as they floated down and kept handing them out after they landed.

Soon, every galumpher had a sandwich, and not long after that...

... there were *no more galumphers*.

"We have mountains of fur in the back yard," yelled Jacob.

"And a whole lot of kids," said Chloe.

"And we have one to take care of in here," said Mom, speaking softly again. "What's your name, sweetie?"

It was Penelope.

Chapter 12. Back to Normal

Almost everyone on the Mainland was watching TV. They all saw the galumphers turn into children as they ate peanut butter sandwiches. Parents from all over spotted their long-lost children who had disappeared years earlier or gotten "lost" on a visit to Galumphagos Island.

None of the children got older while they were missing. "She was six when we lost her 10 years ago," said Penelope's parents when they came to pick her up "and she's six now. She hasn't changed a bit. We're getting her back just where we left off!" It was as if the years that kids spent on the Island never happened.

The Millers became famous for a while. It was exciting for about two days, but having reporters around all the time soon became just another pain on the neck. Mom and Dad were glad when they could go back to work, and the kids were glad to go back to school.

Even Emily. As she entered the lunchroom on her first day back, two of the in-crowd girls grabbed her, one by each arm. "Sit with us, sit with us," they said. They jumped up and down like cheerleaders.

"No thank you," Emily said as she pulled her arms away. She walked over to the table of a girl who was in some of her classes. Like Emily, she always sat alone reading a book during lunchtime.

"Can I have lunch with you?" Emily asked. She pulled out a chair across the table and sat down.

The girl put her book down, looked at Emily, smiled and said "Sure. That would be nice. My name's Jasmine."

"I know," said Emily. "I'm Emily."

"Everyone knows who *you* are!" said Jasmine.

"Maybe," Emily said. "I'm still Emily."

"Everyone says you're about the bravest kid on earth."

"I don't think so," said Emily. What Emily thought was that she'd just been running away. She ran away from the cool crowd and then she ran away from the galumphers. No one ever said it was brave to run away. She didn't want to talk about it.

"Say," Emily said, "do you know that girl sitting behind you?"

Jasmine looked over her shoulder, turned back toward Emily and nodded.

"Let's ask her to sit with us, too, okay?"

Jasmine turned back around, tapped the girl on the shoulder, and then there were three. By the end of the week, there were six. That filled up the table, so six it stayed – six lonely readers who now had a group of friends and who no longer worried about what the cool crowd might do or say or think.

That, Emily thought, was braver than anything else she had done.

Jacob had his own problems. Kids were trying to pick fights with him at school. He told Dad about it one night.

"I'm not surprised," said Dad. "They want to show how tough they are, so they want to whip the kid who whipped the galumphers."

"Well, they're not going to."

"Did you whip them?" Dad asked.

"No," said Jacob. "We didn't fight."

"They'll keep at it," Dad said.

Jacob knew that but he wasn't sure what he should do about it. Dad usually didn't have great ideas, but it couldn't hurt to ask him. "What do you think I should do?"

"I don't know," Dad said.

That was different. Dad used to think that he always knew what to do.

"But," Dad went on, "I'm pretty sure that you're smart enough and grown up enough to figure it out for yourself."

Jacob stopped and thought. "I think I just won't fight them," he said.

"You'll get teased," Dad said. "Kids will call you a chicken."

"I know," Jacob said. "I don't have to show anyone how tough I am."

"No," Dad said, "you sure don't."

As for Chloe, she didn't just draw pretty things any more. Now, when she drew a field of flowers, some of them had broken stems. When she drew a pretty bird, it would be chasing a pretty butterfly or getting chased by a hawk.

At the end of school one day, her teacher told her to go to the principal's office. Mom, Dad and the school art teacher were sitting around a table with the principal.

"Did I do something wrong?" Chloe asked.

The art teacher took three of Chloe's drawings out of a folder and put them down on the table. "Chloe," she said, "I've been telling your parents how interesting your art work has become. I think it's quite wonderful. Do you know what the word 'prodigy' means?"

"Sort of," said Chloe.

"It means...." The art teacher stopped. She seemed stumped. "It means we all think you should get special art training."

"If you want to," added Mom.

"But," the principal said, "we're wondering why you started drawing pictures like this after you came back."

Chloe didn't wonder at all. She knew exactly why. "I always wanted to draw pictures like that," she said, "but I was afraid."

"I don't understand," the principal said. "What were you afraid of?"

Chloe looked around the room at each adult, one at a time, eye to eye.

"Us," Dad said. "She was afraid of us."

"She was afraid that, if she drew pictures like that, we'd do exactly what we're doing," Mom said. "We'd make a big deal about it. We'd worry there was something wrong with her. We might even tell her to keep drawing nice pretty pictures when what she really wanted to do was make necklaces from grass."

"Necklaces from grass?" said the principal. "I don't see what that's got to do with anything."

"I do," said Chloe. "When can I start art classes?"

Years later, when she was grown up and had children of her own, Chloe always remembered that very moment as the time when she became an artist.

And Then...

Then the oddest thing happened. Galumphagos Island disappeared. It didn't sink into the sea. The ocean scientists said they would have been able to tell if that had happened. It just vanished. No one knew where or how. Even Professor Chuckles was stumped.

In time, everyone forgot about the galumphers and Galumphagos Island. The tapes of TV news reports and the words in old newspapers all changed. None of them said anything about galumphers or the Island or the invasion. There were no DVDs or internet, because this all happened too long ago.

Even the kids who had been galumphers did not remember a thing about it. Everyone in the world forgot.

Everyone except five people named Emily, Chloe, Jacob, Mom and Dad. They never spoke about it, though, because they thought it would be best to let the memories disappear just as the Island itself did. That's why you've never heard of Galumphagos Island before.

Lately, though, they decided they could tell you about it because, with the passing of time, no one would believe it really happened anyway.

You'd think it was just a story.

About the Artist

Ellen C. Maze is a best-selling author, a fine artist, and publisher based out of North Alabama. Her artwork is sold worldwide and hung in various private collections throughout the South. Ellen specializes in animal portraiture and children's book illustration. Her house has two cats, and one of them likes to rub noses.

CPSIA information can be obtained at www.ICGtesting.com
Printed in the USA
LVOW01s2145120214

373519LV00009B/140/P